Who Turned Up the Heat?

Eco-Pig Explains Global Warming

By Lisa S. French

Illustrations by Barry Gott

visit us at www.abdopublishing.com

For George—LSF

Published by Magic Wagon, a division of the ABDO Group, 8000 West 78th Street, Edina, Minnesota 55439.

Printed in the United States.

 Manufactured with paper containing at least 10% post-consumer waste

Text by Lisa S. French
Illustrations by Barry Gott
Edited by Stephanie Hedlund and Rochelle Baltzer
Interior layout and design by Nicole Brecke
Cover design by Nicole Brecke

Library of Congress Cataloging-in-Publication Data
French, Lisa S.
  Who turned up the heat? : Eco-Pig explains global warming / by Lisa S. French ; illustrated by Barry Gott.
     p. cm. — (Eco-Pig)
  Summary: In rhyming text, Eco-Pig explains what global warming does to the earth and how everyone can help.
  ISBN 978-1-60270-664-4
  [1. Stories in rhyme. 2. Pigs—Fiction. 3. Global warming—Fiction. 4. Green movement—Fiction.] I. Gott, Barry, ill. II. Title.
  PZ8.3.F9085Wo 2009
  [E]—dc22
                            2008055337

On top of a mountain
at the edge of a sea
lives an Earth-loving pig
in a town called To-Be.

His name is Bernard
but please call him E.P.,
should you visit his home
in the green apple tree.

From his Eco-Pig nest,
tenth branch from the bottom,
he keeps an eye on our planet,
winter, spring, summer, and autumn.

5

On the first day of March,
not quite yet spring,
E.P. was recycling,
his most favorite thing.

As he sorted out cans
he stopped and he thought,
*My goodness, my snout
is unusually hot.*

7

It was hot to the touch
and blinking bright red.
So were the ears
on top of his head.

A sunburn in March?
How could this be?
It just snowed yesterday.
Earth is singing off-key.

9

"And have you noticed," cried Lou,
"the tulips are out,
and the red-breasted robins
are hopping about?

"From winter to summer?
This much I know,
there should be four seasons.
Now where did they go?"

11

"Earth's running a fever," E.P. agreed.
"We've cranked up the heat!
It's called global warming,
so not cool and not neat.

"We turn on all our lights,
and we drive and we fly.
But I'm starting to wonder
what we've done to the sky.

13

"When we power the planet
we need to be fair!
Burning oil and coal
puts greenhouse gas in the air.

"Some gas gets swallowed
by our oceans and trees.
But we're making too much
and they're starting to wheeze.

15

"This bad gas we can't see
traps the heat from the sun.
Then Earth gets too hot,
like a grilled burger, no bun.

"If Earth's temperature rises
by just one small degree,
that means really big changes
for the land and the sea!"

"Just one degree?" asked Lou.
"Is that such a big deal?
Are you sure, E.P.?
Is this warming for real?"

E.P. replied, "Keeping the climate
in balance is part of nature's big plan.
Everyone knows
pigs aren't meant to be tan!

19

"Plus, glaciers are melting,
which puts our friends underwater,
and that sure doesn't work,
unless you're an otter.

"While some places flood," E.P. cried,
"others will fry.
Our fruits and our veggies
could just curl up and die.

"To get Earth back in tune,
we need to go Green.
We need to start now,
if you know what I mean!"

Electric power and cars
warm the planet the most.
If we don't use them less,
then our climate is toast!

23

If you don't have to go far,
ride the bus or your bike.
Need to go to the store?
Take your dog for a hike!

For a major road trip,
why not share a ride?
You'll make some new friends,
and show your Earth pride.

We can learn to make power
from the wind and the sun.
It's renewable and clean.
Plus, wind farms are fun!

Let's switch off and unplug
the things we don't need.
We'll reduce greenhouse gas.
On this we're agreed!

If we each cut back a little,

it will add up to a lot.

Let's pitch in and help out

before our home gets too hot!

Let's give back to our planet,
not always subtract.
Because what we do matters,
and that is a fact!

Words to Know

global warming—refers to an average increase in the Earth's temperature, which in turn causes changes in climate.

Green—related to or being protective of the environment.

greenhouse gas—any gas that traps radiation (heat from the sun) in Earth's atmosphere.

recycle—to break down waste, glass, or cans so they can be used again.

renewable energy—energy made from natural resources such as sunlight and wind which are naturally replaced.

wind farm—a group of machines that convert wind into electrical energy.

Did You Know?

- The temperature of Earth has increased by one degree Fahrenheit over the past century. Scientists expect the average temperature of Earth to increase another two to six degrees over the next century.

- Climate change can affect ocean levels, our crops, the air, and the water.

- Rapid climate change does not give Earth's plants and animals enough time to adapt, putting some species at risk for extinction.

- The number of heat waves, strong tropical storms, and wildfires may increase due to global warming.

- One way to fight global warming is to use fewer fossil fuels. Fossil fuels, such as coal and oil, are formed from the remains of prehistoric animals and plants. Energy formed from the wind and sun are better for our environment.

More Ways to Reduce Global Warming!

Talk to your mom and dad about
what you can try at home:

1. Carpool to school and after-school activities.
2. Use public transportation.
3. Ride a bicycle or walk to nearby places.
4. Recycle paper, plastic, glass, and metals.
5. Clean your room and donate gently used clothing and toys to those in need.
6. Unplug the television and the computer when not in use.
7. Turn off lights when you leave a room.